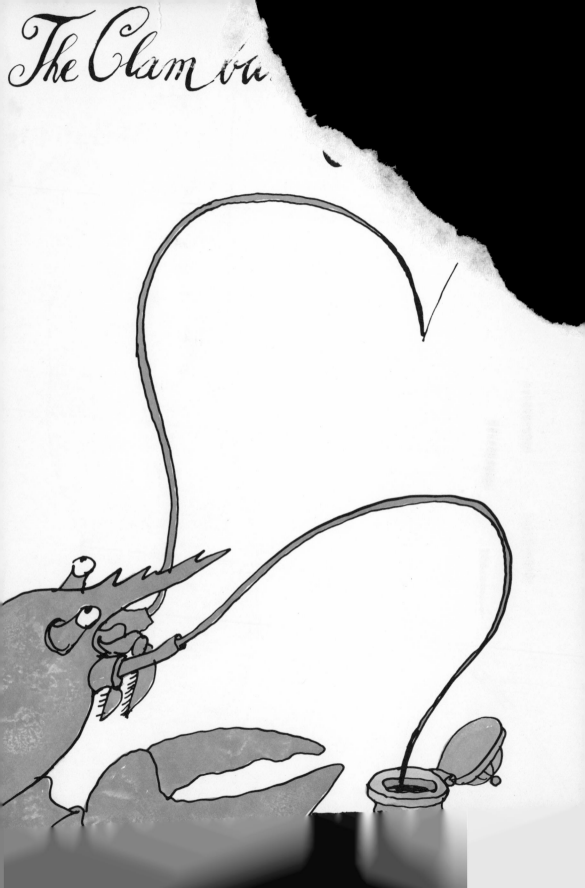

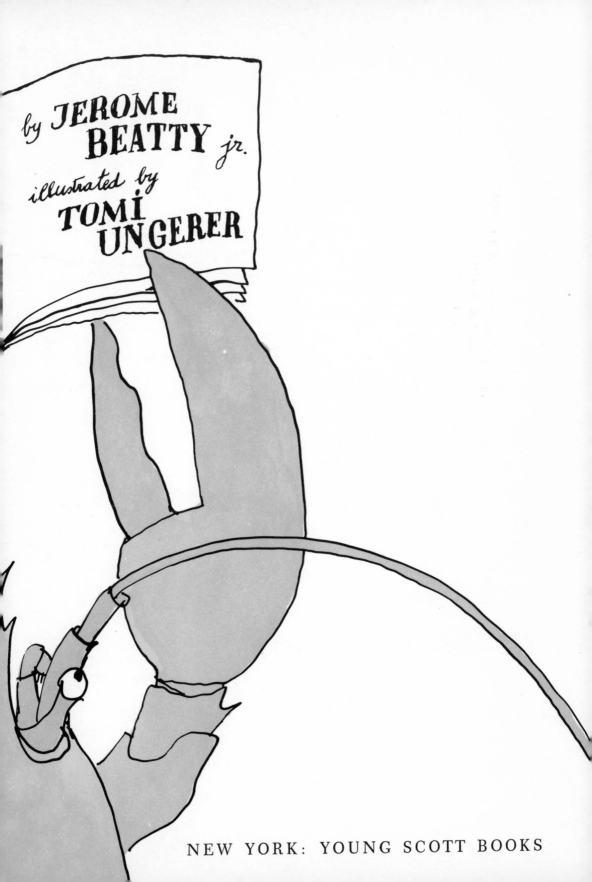

by JEROME BEATTY jr.

illustrated by TOMI UNGERER

NEW YORK: YOUNG SCOTT BOOKS

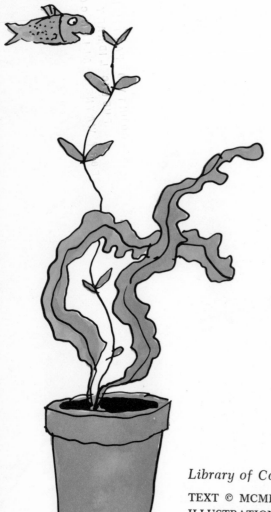

FOR JANE

One delightfully cold day Daniel Lobster scurried along the bottom of the Atlantic Ocean near his favorite hangout, Monhegan Island. He was looking for breakfast. His eye fell upon a juicy soft-shell clam hiding under a rock.

Daniel was four years old and very hungry, as any growing arthropod would be at that time of the day. He waved his crushing claw ahead of him, preparing to seize the doomed bivalve. At that moment, though, he was startled to hear shouting. He paused and listened.

7

"Come to our assistance!" a voice gurgled.
"Help! Help!" others were crying.

Daniel turned his antennae and then his
eyes in the direction of the sounds, but he
could not feel or see anything through the
murky waters. He went back to the clam, but
the wily little thing had escaped into the sand.

Angry with himself for losing out on such
a tasty tidbit, Daniel made up his mind to find
out what caused the yelling that had spoiled
his breakfast.

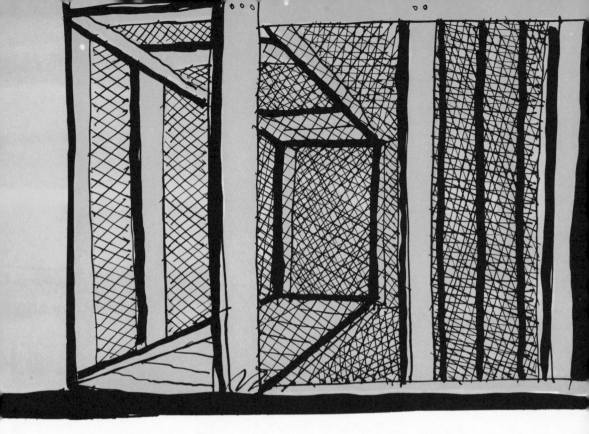

"I'll come back later and catch that slippery clam," he promised. He moved toward the hubbub, his curiosity getting the better of his hunger pangs for the moment.

Soon he came upon a sight that made his heart thump faster against his shell. It was a huge structure of wood and wire. Inside were several lobsters. Some tore and clawed at the box in a vain attempt to get out. Others just sat unhappily. A few children seemed unaware of their plight; they played tag.

9

Daniel realized he was face to face with an object he had been hearing about all his life, but which he had never seen.

"So this is a lobster trap," he thought. "This is the mysterious thing that comes down from above, and which all lobsters are supposed to keep away from."

It was not a pleasant picture, all those poor innocent inhabitants of the ocean floor, his own kind, caught there and destined for some unknown fate. Daniel felt sorry for them.

Just then he was surprised to hear his name called.

"Dan! Dan, my boy! It's me, your Uncle Chris!" Daniel peered through the bars. It was his uncle, all right. "Run! Get help before it's too late!" the prisoner cried.

10

The young fellow turned and propelled himself home as fast as he could go. He bumped
over rocks and pushed through weeds, his
swimmerets flapping at high speed. Finally he
reached the door of the cave where he lived.

"Mom! Mom!" he cried as he pushed his way inside. "There's trouble over at Monhegan! Uncle Chris—the others—!" Daniel had to stop to catch his breath.

A huge figure appeared. It was Mrs. Lobster. "Now, son, calm down and tell me what this is all about."

Her son explained the situation, and she said, "Oh, no, not Chris!" She sat down, put her head in her claws, and sobbed softly.

"Mom," Daniel said excitedly, "Uncle Chris wanted us to help him. What can we do?"

Mrs. Lobster looked up. "There's nothing we can do, son. Your Uncle was just calling for help instinctively. He knows there's only one escape from the trap, and it isn't anything we lobsters can control. Oh, Chris, oh—oh!" She sobbed some more.

While Daniel tried to comfort his mother, there was a sound at the door, and Mr. Lobster came in, carrying some snails for lunch.

"Why, Laura," he said, "you're crying. What's the matter?"

"They got Chris," she cried. "My own brother. Ten years without going near a trap, and now—"

"Well, I'll be darned," her husband whispered in disbelief. He flopped down in his rocky chair. "The poor guy. When did it happen? How did you find out?"

"Daniel saw him. He's over near Monhegan. Hoo-hoo-hoo." She dissolved in tears again.

Mr. Lobster jumped up. "Well, let's get over there. Maybe they'll throw him back down."

"Don't be silly, George. He's ten pounds if he's an ounce, and you know it."

"It won't hurt to go see what this is all about. Come on."

14

Daniel soon led the family to the spot. As they came closer they saw that a big crowd had gathered.

"The usual gang of busybodies," Mr. Lobster mumbled. "Let us through! We've got relatives in there." He pinched his way through the throng, leading his wife and son. And there was Uncle Chris behind the bars.

"Oh, Chris, how could you?" his sister asked.

The captive looked sheepish. "I don't know. I was rushing around searching for some breakfast and there was the most marvelous smell of stale herring, and the next thing I knew—I was inside here."

While Daniel wondered what could be done to save the helpless group, his mother grabbed him by the legs and pulled him around to another side of the contraption. She pointed at a hole in the wire. It made an entrance into the trap.

"See that? Now don't you ever go near one of these things. That's how your uncle and all the others got caught today, and how many of

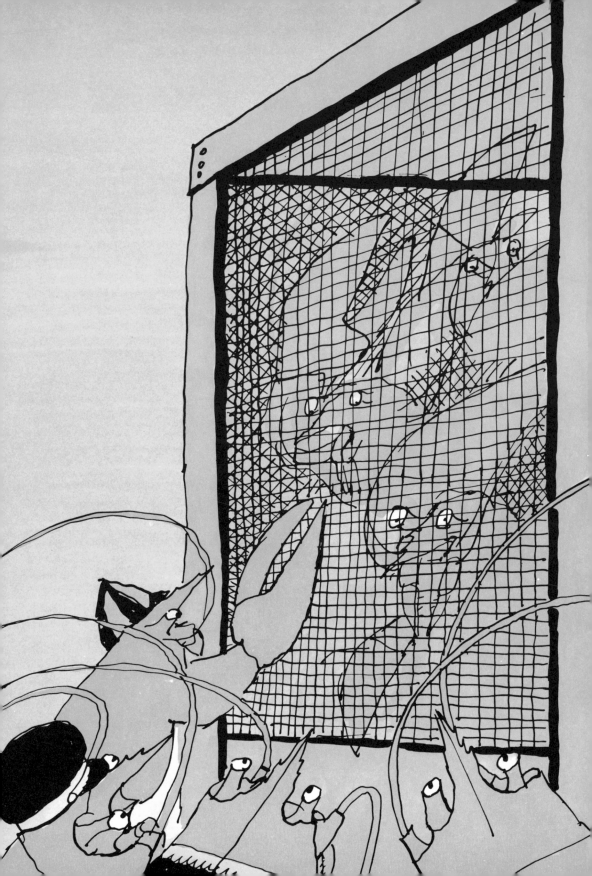

our long-lost friends and neighbors have been caught in the past."

"Gee, Mom, why don't they just come out the same way they went in?"

"Because, you foolish boy, the hole gets smaller and smaller as you go through. You can squeeze in but you can't squeeze out."

Daniel and his mother drifted back to the spot where Uncle Chris and George Lobster were talking.

"Hang on, Chris," Daniel's father was saying. "I'll try to nip through here." He raised his big pincers.

Chris looked grateful, but he said, "Nice try, George. It'll never work, of course." At that moment there was a movement and the whole box lurched and left the bottom. All the prisoners were thrown off their feet as the trap went up, up, up and out of sight above. There was much weeping and wailing and shouting of goodbye.

"We'll wait for you, darling!" one mother called.

Part of the mob left, but some stayed on,

their eyes and feelers straining upward into the gloom. For what seemed a long time, nothing happened, but then a tiny object came into view. It seesawed back and forth and appeared larger. Then Daniel saw with surprise it was one of the youngsters who had been playing tag. He landed on the bottom and his mother rushed to greet him with cries of happiness.

"How come?" Daniel asked.

"The small ones always come back," his mother replied sadly. Her eyes were still glued to the blackness above, looking for Chris. More little kids sailed into view, but that was all. Soon all was quiet.

"Come on," Mr. Lobster said. "We'd better get out of here before—" He glanced up at a huge shadow that formed over their heads and loomed ever closer. "Watch out! Here she comes!"

The two parents took hold of their boy, and all three swam and ran full speed for the protection of a nearby ledge. They peered out in time to see the lobster trap come crashing

20

down onto almost the same spot from which
it had left a few minutes before. It sat there,
a silent reminder of the missing Uncle Chris.

"Sometimes," Mr. Lobster said quietly, "people who have kept out of the trap have been
crushed when it came back down."

That night the family sat at dinner and talked about the day's events. Daniel, of course, had heard about the traps all his life, but he had always obeyed his parents and had never gone near one. Now, however, he wanted to know all about them. His father explained.

"Children find it hard to keep away from the delicious food inside the traps. Grownups with any sense know the danger, but sometimes when you're hungry, and you're cruising along the bottom seeking a meal, you unconsciously scoot right through one of those terrible entrances before you know it. That's what must have happened to Chris."

"The sad thing is," his mother remarked, "that the young ones are returned from above each time, so they begin to think it's all right to go in and get the delicious morsels. Then one day—they just don't come back. That's usually when they're about five years old, right in the prime of their youth."

"Yeah," Daniel said. "A guy in my class named Pete Prawn used to go in a trap on a

dare, and he kept winning until one day he didn't float back down. I wonder what it is like — up there." Dan's eyes turned toward the ceiling.

"Well, enough young people have returned —including your father—so that we have a pretty good idea."

"You went up in a trap?"

"Yup. I was a foolish one in those days. To tell the truth, it's about the most exciting experience I've ever had. That's why a lot of lobsters get caught. There's a strange fascination to the trap that somehow blinds them to the dangers. In my case, I found myself up out of the water with a large, white animal of some sort grabbing me and sizing me up. All my older companions he had tossed into a pile. Me, he tossed back into the water. I wasn't big enough. It was a lot of fun, but I wouldn't do it again."

"And what happens to the big ones in that pile?"

George Lobster shrugged his appendages. "Who knows?"

24

Daniel thought this over a minute. Then he asked, "Would I be thrown back?"

His father's eyes popped, and his mother let out a little scrurgle (which is halfway between a scream and a gurgle).

"Daniel!" she cried. "What are you saying?"

"Don't get any ideas, son. As you are now, you would probably be rejected. But you are awfully close to the line, and it just wouldn't be worth taking any chances."

But that night as he lay on his bed of kelp and tried to sleep, Daniel thought about it. He remembered that at least three of the youths who had come floating back down that morning were larger than he. Any dummy could figure out that under those circumstances he, Daniel, would also be tossed back. He slapped one claw against the other and made up his mind to enter the trap deliberately.

"Maybe I'll get a chance to look around and see what's happened to Uncle Chris before they toss me back into the water."

Early the next day he scratched out a note on an old shell: "Dear Folks—Have gone to

look for Uncle Chris. Don't worry about me. Your son, D."

He sneaked into the kitchen, packed a plankton sandwich, and tiptoed out of the house before his mother and father were awake. He made his way through the cold waters toward Monhegan Island. It grew lighter as he climbed the incline; eventually he heard a clamor similar to that of the day before. He neared the fatal spot and, sure enough, looming before him was the wood

and wire structure. Already some children had
been enticed inside; they were having a fine
time eating the good food they found there,
little realizing the adventure that lay ahead.

As he was hesitating, he heard a voice.
"Watch out, young fellow. This is no place
for you."

It was an old lady who had been trapped. Daniel ignored her warning and went closer to the entrance. An unusual sense of excitement surged through his ganglia. He paused at the opening as the old female tried to wave him off. His nerve left him for a moment, but in a last burst of courage he swam boldly toward the narrow opening. He easily forced his way into the cage.

30

"Well, now, ye silly boy," the old lady cackled. "Ye've gone and done it."

Daniel felt very sure of himself. "Don't worry, ma'am. I can take care of myself."

"Oh, can ye, now?" she said in a mocking tone. "I suppose yer one of these juvenile delinquents thinks he's going to get thrown back in the water after a little joy ride in the trap, eh?"

Daniel smiled. He grabbed a few pieces of herring and swallowed them. A few more lobsters came into the trap, not listening to the shouts of the old female. The smell of the fish was just too good. Yet, some older and smarter folks remained outside watching. If the old lady was so smart, Daniel wondered, how come she was inside, herself? He was about to ask her when there was a terrible jolt. He felt himself pulled dizzily through the water. In a second the bottom of the sea and the curiosity seekers were lost to sight.

"See you later!" Daniel called gaily. It was lots of fun.

A moment later, with a roar, the water just

disappeared. It got very bright and Daniel had to shade his eyes with his claw. The whole trap was opened and all the prisoners were dumped out together in a bruising mass. Daniel looked at his captors. They were sure funny things, with only four legs, no feelers, and little tiny claws.

With these little claws the white creatures picked up the lobsters one by one. Some went into another pile and some went over the side.

"Well, I've seen all I want to," Daniel told himself, as he was roughly grabbed and lifted high. "Hurry up. Toss me back."

But Daniel was in for the surprise of his life. The big ugly head of his captor was close to his, and a stick was held against his back for a moment. And Daniel was not tossed into the water, but was thrown onto the pile. He landed right on top of the old female.

"Ouch!" she cried. "Well, it's my brash friend. How do you like *this* joy ride, eh?"

"I'm too small!" Daniel called out. "Send me back home!"

"It's not your weight, fella, it's your length

that counts," she told him. "And you look right long for your age."

Daniel was stunned. He hardly noticed that other lobsters landed on top of him. He thought sadly, "Well, I may still find out what happened to Uncle Chris, even if I never get back to tell anyone about it."

Daniel found he couldn't think very clearly any more. The lack of water was making him drowsy, and soon he dozed off, as did all the others in the same fix as he. He dreamed of home. He was awakened by a terrible feeling of falling; he found himself splashing into water again, along with his other unfortunate cellmates. It wasn't the Atlantic Ocean, though; it was a large tank from which there was no escape. There were already many imprisoned lobsters there, and more kept coming in after Daniel's party arrived. There was an awful racket as everybody kept up a loud gurgling and talking, kicking and pushing impolitely in the overcrowded quarters.

Daniel reached out to pinch one rude fellow when he found to his horror that his claws were locked shut! A tough band had been put around them and he was helpless. He observed that the same fate had befallen the others. This was very bad news, for a lobster is completely defenseless without his weapons, which also serve as his means of gathering food.

"Oh, my," Daniel said. "If I don't get chewed up I'll starve." Then he brightened up. "Maybe I can find Uncle Chris."

Fully awake now, the young adventurer turned his feelers this way and that, bumping his useless claws against other lobsters, big and small. He stopped a young one who was hurrying past.

"Have you seen my Uncle Chris?" he asked him.

"How would I know?" the other answered grumpily. "What does he look like?"

"Well, he's about fifteen years old. He has a scar on his third left leg. His full name is Christopher Carapace and his address is 44 Coral Road, Monhegan Depths, North Atlantic."

"No, never heard of him. I got my own problems. I'm only four years old. Should have been thrown back. I don't know what's gotten into these people, they—"

Daniel mumbled his thanks and quickly moved away, not wishing to hear any more of the story which sounded like his own experience. He shoved his way through the crowds for some time until he came upon a familiar figure: the old lady who had been captured along with him. He then saw with a pleasant surprise that she was chatting with none other than his uncle!

"Uncle Chris!"

"Daniel! How in the world—?"

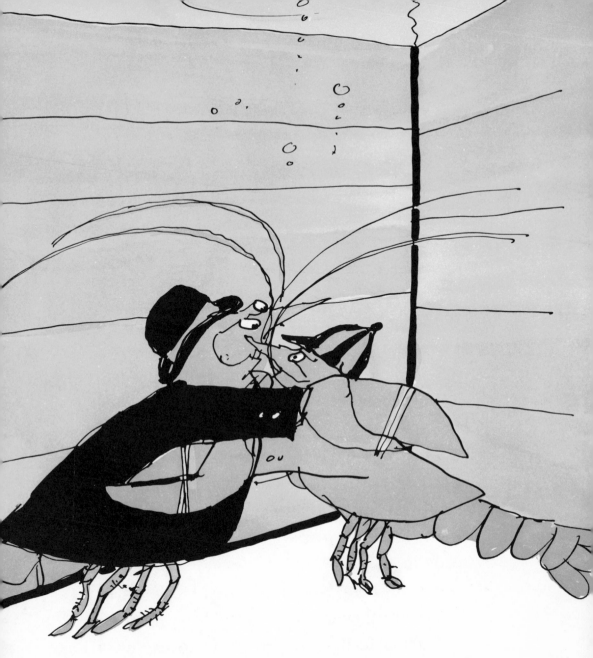

They fell into each other's claws. Daniel
was happy to see his favorite uncle. He told
him about his experiences.

"This is your nephew?" the old lady asked. "I told him to keep out of the trap." She began explaining to Uncle Chris what had happened.

"How come *you* got caught?" Daniel blurted out.

"Oh, these eyes aren't what they used ter be, sonny. I just blundered into this predicament. Got no real complaints, though. Lived twenty-one full years. Granny Crustacean is ready to go."

"To go where, Granny?" asked Uncle Chris. "What are they going to do with us now?"

"I got a feeling they're going to eat us. I don't know why. I just got the feeling. And when Granny Crustacean gets a feeling, it's usually right."

38

"So that's it, is it?" Chris murmured sadly.

"But why?" Daniel cried. "I'm sure we don't taste very good. They're cannibals, that's what! Eating poor defenseless lobsters! We're not food!"

"Not quite right, son," his uncle observed philosophically. "All life is the story of the hunter and the hunted. You yourself pursue the lowly clam, do you not? These white creatures are now doing the same to us. And I am sure that someplace—farther than we can see—there are even higher animals that prey upon these ugly white-faced beings that have captured us."

"Your uncle's right," added Granny. "I've learned that much about life; you've got to take the bitter with the sweet."

Daniel was silent, thinking about all the sweet things in his past—the long summer days with no school, Mom's homemade fish chowder, the thrill of shedding your first skin.

"I'm too young to die," he said firmly. "It's the job of the hunted to escape from the hunter. There are plenty of clams that got away from me, and maybe today there'll be a lobster who gets away from these—"

He never did finish his threat. Right before his eyes Uncle Chris disappeared. In his place there was a swirl of bubbles. Daniel looked up and saw feet and tail pop out of sight. Before he could get over his shock, the same thing happened to Granny Crustacean: she was gone.

Then a powerful grip on his own waist and Daniel went flying after them. He felt airsick as he was tossed this way and that, landing in a squirming pile of other lobsters, and then being jounced and bounced for what seemed a long, long time.

"Daniel, are you there?" a voice cried.

"Yes, I'm here, Uncle Chris," he replied.

"Good boy! Keep a stiff upper mandible."

As before, Daniel grew drowsy from lack of water. How long he slept he didn't know. He was dreaming about the time he scored two eels for Monhegan Depths Low School in the big game against Penobscot Bay. The game went on and on. He was being tackled

over and over again when he slowly came
back to his senses; it was Uncle Chris nudg-
ing him.

"Wake up, Dan," he whispered.

The youngster lifted his head and looked
about. He and all the other lobsters were con-
fined in a basket of some sort. They peered
through the cracks in the side. It was dark
except for a strong light that blazed in the dis-

tance. Several of the funny-looking creatures
with the white faces and no feelers milled
around the area. They seemed to be pushing
stones into a hole in the ground.

"Where are we?"

"We're on a beach somewhere," Uncle Chris
replied. He waved a feeler. "There's the ocean

43

over there. I watched them. They dug into the sand. They picked up seaweed. They've got clams and some other stuff. I don't know what it's all about."

"Granny knows," said a quiet voice behind them. They turned to hear more. "It's what they call a clambake. I heard about it when I was a little girl."

"It's getting warm," Chris said.

"That's the fire." She pointed to the blazing in the distance.

The three watched as the creatures rolled more stones from the fire into the depression in the sand.

"Those must be hot," Daniel said.

The whites tossed seaweed over the stones, followed by various green, yellow and brown objects and more seaweed. Smoke began to rise from the pile.

"They put some food on there, I guess," Chris remarked. "But seaweed isn't very tasty."

"Clams are, though," Daniel said. He thought a minute. "Say, if they were going to

44

cook lobsters, they'd call it a lobster bake, not a clambake."

No one answered, because they didn't really believe it. There was silence in the basket, except for the glug-glug of crustaceans trying to breathe air. The quiet was broken by a cry from one of those in the rear who couldn't see.

"Why don't they do something?" was the hysterical shout. "What's next?"

The response came immediately. Daniel was first. A white-face grabbed him and all his fellow captives and placed them on the seaweed. It was warm. Then more things were piled on top of them. It was getting hotter and hotter. Daniel's stomach was uncomfortable. He reached out with his claw and cut away a big piece of weed that hung in front of his eyes.

It was a few seconds before he understood what this meant. Somehow the band had come off and one claw was free. Well, he thought, maybe I am going to get out of this one. The star greenback of Monhegan Depths Low School still has a fighting chance!

He plucked the band off his other claw. He pushed his way through the mass of weeds and steam, calling for Uncle Chris. He soon came face to face with him.

"Here, quick!" He clipped the two bands off his uncle's tremendous pincer and crusher. "Let's make a crawl for it!"

Uncle Chris opened and closed his claws to get the stiffness out of them. "Good boy!" he cried. "But what about the others?"

"Ask them to come along."

Uncle Chris called out. "It's me, Chris Carapace. My nephew Daniel and I are forcing our way to freedom. If you're game, follow me!"

There were shouts and murmurs, followed by rustling and crackling as the lobsters pushed their way toward the sound of the voice. They held out their claws and were clipped free. Soon all their pincers and crushers were unhampered.

"All right, let's go," said Uncle Chris. He started pushing his way through the jungle, with Daniel on his tail and Granny Crustacean right behind. The rest of the gang followed.

46

A hot brown object fell on Daniel's head. He
brushed it aside. The steam got in his eyes
and bothered his feelers. It was rough going.
Finally Uncle Chris stopped so suddenly that
Daniel bumped into his tail.

48

"Hold it," the older chap said. "We're about to come out into the open." He carefully peeked through the tangle of seaweed. "They're all over there by the fire. Quietly now. Head for the water."

He crawled down the sandy beach, followed by Daniel and the others, one by one. It was not as easy as swimming through the water, but by digging in with his eight legs, Daniel found he could move rather well. They had not gone far when Uncle Chris stationed Daniel at the side of the route and told him to keep the line moving in the right direction.

"I'll be down at the water," he said. Daniel

took his position. On one side he could hear
the friendly lapping of the waves on the shore;
on the other was the scraping and rustle of
the band of lobsters on their way to freedom.

Daniel was annoyed to see that quite a few
of them were greedy enough to have brought
along with them some of the food that had
been in the clambake. One was carrying a
clam; another dragged some green leaves behind him, and so on.

"You fools!" Daniel whispered. "Your lives
are at stake. You're slowing down the whole
operation this way."

"Mind your own business, buddy," grunted

one young wiseguy through a mouthful of food.

Before Daniel could think of an answer tragedy struck. There was noise up toward the blazing lights; the horrible white creatures were coming his way, each on two of its legs and waving the other two in the air.

"Oh-oh. Here's trouble."

Granny, who had been going by just at this moment, stopped and looked. A few seconds later Uncle Chris appeared. As the white ones came closer, the whole line of escaping lobsters came to a halt, apparently too frightened to move. Daniel wondered if this was the end for all of them. He was jarred from his thoughts by a shout from his uncle.

"Daniel! Granny! This is no time to quit. This is a matter of life or death. Now, Dan, you were a Bay Scout, so you can give orders. Assemble every able-bodied male over there by that rock. And you tell 'em to drop those goodies they're carrying. Granny, see that the women, youngsters, and old folks keep moving toward the ocean. Let's go!"

The three rushed up and down the line, organizing the escapees. Soon the lobsters were divided into two parties. One party was being herded toward the water by Granny Crustacean. The other milled around the rock, until Daniel had them line up and count off.

In the distance the lights flickered, casting spooky shadows on the whole scene. The whites came closer, making weird sounds with their mouths. Their legs were long, each of

them having five wiggly things at the end. When they saw the big crowd of lobsters, they seemed to hesitate a moment. This gave Uncle Chris the time he needed. He climbed onto the rock.

"All right, fellas!" he shouted. "There's no time to waste. Organize into two platoons. Daniel Lobster will lead the first, setting up defensive positions between the enemy and the sea. I'll take the second platoon onto the right flank here. Are there any questions?"

"Yeah, man," called out one beatnik, "what are we supposed to do, tickle 'em to death with our feelers?"

"No, man," Uncle Chris cried back in his commanding voice. "Pinch! Crush! Fight! Now let's move out!"

With a roar, the others waved their claws in the air. Now that these prisoners saw their chance for freedom imperiled, now that their claws were unhampered, they were prepared to fight to the death, if need be. There is nothing braver than an angry lobster, battling for his life and his loved ones. Someone broke into the famous song from "The Vagabond Crustacean" and the others took it up as they split into two groups and went toward the front lines:

"Give me some lobs who are stout-hearted lobs, Who will bite for the right they adore . . ."

Soon Daniel had the First Platoon digging trenches in a line across the beach. As each lobster crouched in his protective spot, Daniel went along giving encouragement and last-minute instructions.

"Don't pinch until you see the whites of their eyes," he reminded his soldiers.

Daniel had a chance to observe the enemy. He noticed that they, too, had divided into two sections. One group, over to one side, was made up of those with long hair on their heads. The others, short-haired, approached the lobsters' defensive line. Slowly they came. Finally one of them reached over and attempted to grab a member of the First Platoon, who opened both claws and snapped them tight on the reacher's wiggling and

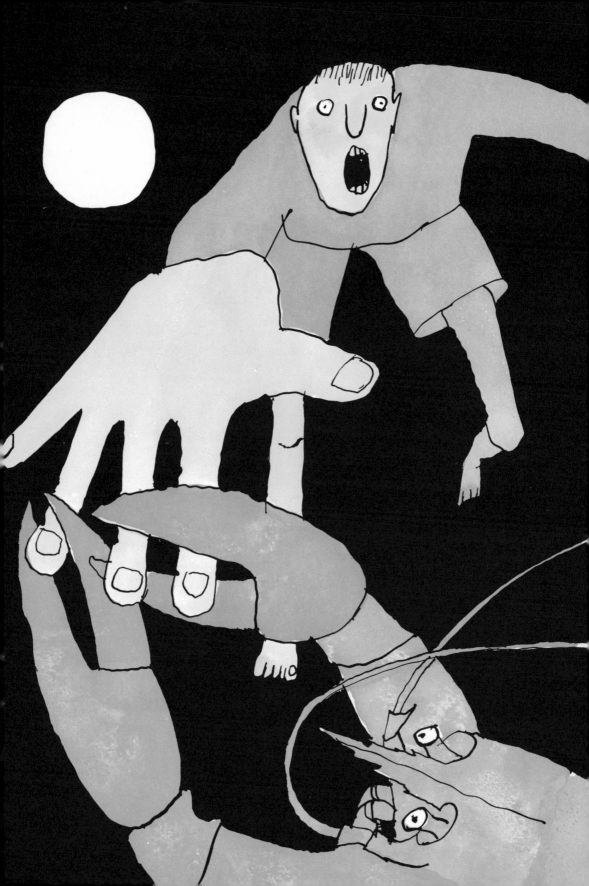

grasping tentacles. There was a loud cry, and
as though it were a signal, the two enemy
lines closed on each other.

"Charge!" Daniel cried. The lobsters
crushed and pinched the ends of the enemy's
legs where they stood in the sand. The noise
was deafening as the click-clack sounded up
and down the beach. The white ones seemed
to fall back, giving Daniel time to look to the
rear and see that Granny and her party were
slipping into the protective ocean waters.

Daniel then turned back to the battle scene. The short-haired platoon was apparently consulting with the long-hairs, who stood in a group near the rock where Uncle Chris had last been seen.

"I wonder what's with the Second Platoon?" Daniel asked himself. "We could really use them as reinforcements, for it appears that the whites are ready to attack once more."

Just as he completed the thought, the whole enemy force seemed to burst into violent action. The loud noises were much more piercing than before; they seemed to come from the mouths of the long-haired ones, who also leaped up and down and sideways in confusion. And then they broke and ran, retreating madly up the beach toward the light. Then Daniel knew where Uncle Chris and his Second Platoon were. It had struck without warning at the unprotected flank of the enemy! The whites retreated as Daniel's platoon cheered.

Uncle Chris and his men moved happily down to meet the others.

"We've won!" someone shouted. The ranks broke and began straggling toward the sea.

"Good work, Uncle," Daniel said.

"Congratulations, Dan. You held them off just perfectly. But we haven't a moment to lose. They will regroup and attack again, I feel sure. Take a squad and bring up the rear as we move away."

"Yes, sir," Daniel replied. He acted on his uncle's orders. His rear guard backed up slowly, keeping an eye on the activity at the enemy camp, as Uncle Chris and the others raced toward the water. Just as he thought they would make it, the whites struck again. This time they came much faster. Daniel looked around and saw that all lobsters were in the water except his little squad. The whites roared and charged.

"Every lobster for himself!" Daniel cried, as he turned and hurried toward the welcome Atlantic Ocean. But he knew he wouldn't make it, for two whites already hovered over him, their grasping tentacles ever closer. Daniel was tired from the long exposure to the air and from the fighting. He shut his eyes, too exhausted to go on, and just waited for the dreadful moment. He heard a few feeble clicks as some of his fellows prepared to fight back, hopeless though the cause might be.

But no rough tentacle grabbed him. Instead, there was a thumping and crashing. Daniel opened his eyes to see the two whites stretched out on all four legs. In a quick glance he saw what had brought them down: they had slipped on the many clams and other foods that the greedy lobsters had dropped there.

In the few extra seconds this gave them,

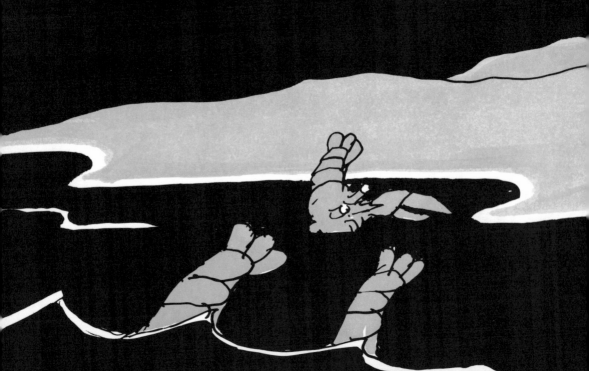

Daniel and his squad scuttled into the waves that washed the sand. "Oh, praise those greedy guys!" he thought gleefully.

Uncle Chris and the others were waiting just beneath the surface. Daniel inhaled the fine salty water and regained his strength.

"That feels good," he breathed.

Then he described to the others what had saved his party at the last minute.

"There's nothing like booby traps to cover a retreat," Uncle Chris commented. "Although I'd rather say we didn't retreat—we just advanced in a different direction."

"Uncle," Daniel smiled, "watch that word 'trap,' will you? It makes me a little bit nervous."

Now Uncle Chris spoke to the entire assemblage. "Folks," he said, "you have just made lobster history. Never before has there been a mass escape of this kind. Now, back to Monhegan Depths to show our friends and relatives we are safe." Everyone clapped claws, and the happy group swam toward their village.

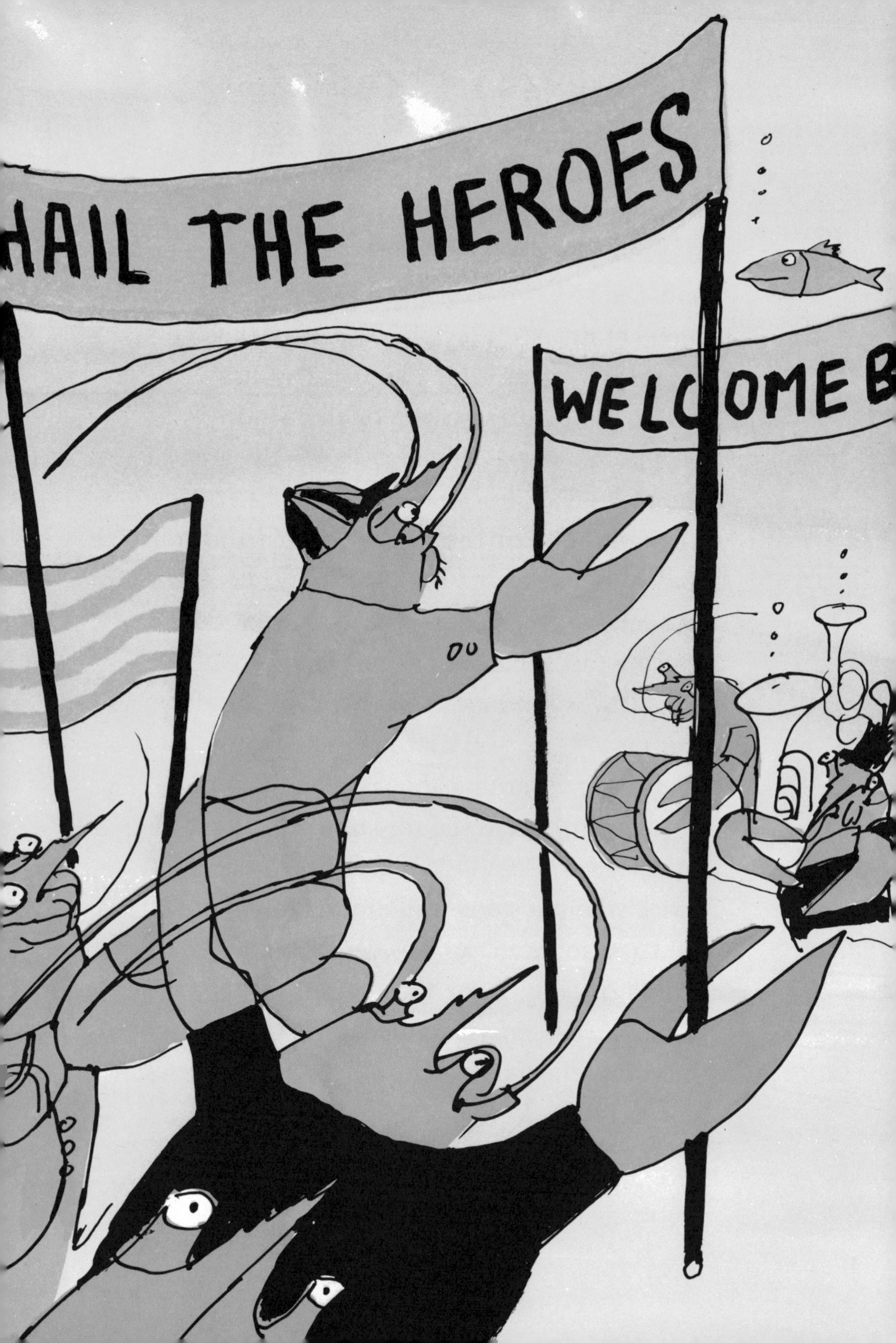
HAIL THE HEROES
WELCOME B

And so it was that Monhegan Depths witnessed one of its wildest celebrations. Daniel's parents were overjoyed to have him and Uncle Chris come back, and they were proud of the part they played in what was now being known as The Clambake Mutiny.

But the greatest effect of the Mutiny was on the life of the inhabitants of that area of the ocean floor. For the first time, lobsters now knew the fate of those who entered the trap and were not tossed back in the water. Great publicity was given to the clambake details and to the behavior of the white creatures. The Town Committee got a full report from the mutineers, and a whole new set of laws was made regarding the trap.

Every day when the trap hit the bottom, the Monhegan Depths Protective Association quickly built a stone wall around it and posted sentries to keep all residents and unwary travelers away from the danger area.

This went on for quite a while until one morning the empty trap didn't come back down again.

About the Author and Artist

The ability to look at life through the antennae of a lobster is one thing Jerome Beatty, Jr., and Tomi Ungerer have in common. Mr. Beatty, born and brought up in the New York and New England area, attended Dartmouth College, worked on newspapers and magazines, and finally settled down in Connecticut as a free-lance writer. Mr. Ungerer, from Alsace, was the scion of a renowned family that had made famous clocks for centuries. As a young man he left home, walked all over Europe, and ended up in New York some ten years ago carrying samples of his art work which, he was told, was "ahead of its time."

Mr. Beatty, a rebel at heart, and Mr. Ungerer, a rebel in deed, first met then. They became friends, helping each other in their work but never actually collaborating until Mr. Ungerer illustrated an adult book of Mr. Beatty's in 1963. Now they have come together to create *The Clambake Mutiny* which they both believe is considerably more than an anthropomorphic tale for the entertainment of children.

This is Jerome Beatty's third children's book. He is known for his adult books as well as his regular "Trade Winds" column in *The Saturday Review*. Tomi Ungerer, a brilliant satirist in his own right, has written and illustrated some of the most popular children's books published in recent years.